MW00876769

Dear Bunny,

Thank you so
much! Live always
shining!
in faith, hope, and love!

Kiki
2009

Islands of Hope

Written by **Kiki Latimer**

Islands of Hope
Author: Kiki Latimer
Illustrations: Franceska Schifrin
Cover design and page layout: Nathalie Jn Baptiste
© Copyright 2009, Kiki Latimer

For information, please contact:

Educa Vision Inc.,
7550 NW 47th Avenue
Coconut Creek, FL 33073
Telephone: 954-968-7433
Fax: 954-970-0330
www.educavision.com

ISBN 13: 978-1-58432-558-1

This book is dedicated to
the people of Bord de Mer, Cap Haitien, Haiti,
The people of the Church of San Joseph's,
Hope Valley, Rhode Island
And
Food for the Poor, the organization
that brought them all together
in this mission of Hope.

∽∾

Special thanks to my friend and editor
Don Kirk,
To my friends and project co-chairs
Maria O'Connor, Emily Naumovski
And
To the inspiration from the person and work
of Dr. Paul Farmer.

In Loving Memory
of
WALTER HABEREK
1924 - 2009

Bonjou. My name is Chante. Mama says that in our language of Kreyol my name means "to sing." I am a little girl with big brown eyes and very dark brown skin. My hair is brown too. When I was little the ends of my hair would turn orange. Mama says that this was because I didn't get enough food to eat. Mama says that when there is no food to eat we must fill ourselves with the old songs. Mama and Papa say that they named me Chante so that we would never lose these songs. The songs are from far far away. I have never been far far away. I have always been here.

Here is the little island country called
Haiti where I live with my Mama and
Papa. We live in a town by the ocean
called Bord de Mer. Papa and I often
walk to the seashore. I pick up shells
and starfish and look out
over the sea.

Papa says that this is a famous place because Christopher Columbus landed here in 1492. If it weren't for him, Papa says that we would still live far far away in Africa. He always seems a little bit sad and yet a little bit proud when he tells me this story.

Papa says that my great great great Grandpa was cruelly taken from his home in Africa, brought here, made a slave in the sugar cane fields. I have tasted sugar cane a few times; it is sweet and woody and juicy. I can make a small piece last all day. It makes my warm fingers sticky and sweet and I think about my great great great Grandpa working in the hot sweet fields. Papa and I walk home together from the sea. We sing the old songs and laugh in the strong hot sun.

When I was very very little we lived in another place. It was a small hut village east of here. Our house was small and made out of old boards and big pieces of rusted brown metal that Papa had found at the dump. It was our own little place and I was happy there. Sometimes Mama cooked dark beans and rice in the big pot on the fire. The deep smell of the beans made my mouth water as I waited. Later the beans would be warm in my mouth and the rice would be sticky on my fingers and I would lick them.

But most nights there was no dinner and I would just wait for the sun to set. Then I would feel the ache in my tummy. I know this made Mama sad. On these nights she would often give me one of the five cent market cookies made of dried yellow dirt, shortening and salt. They took away the empty ache in my tummy but filled my mouth with dryness.

Later I would look out through the crack in the boards and watch the stars come out one by one. I listened to the sounds of the dark warm night, the close chirp of crickets and katydids and the far off sounds of deep drumming prayers. Outside deep and soft like the prayer drums, I would hear Papa gently singing the old songs from far far away. Chante. Chante. Mama whispers my name goodnight. The night is long and warm.

At the tail end of the darkness a rooster's crow breaks the stillness. In the morning light I would sit on my mat and push my heels against the hard stony dirt floor. Sometimes with a sharp stick I make designs in the dirt. Mama always likes my drawings in the dirt. She says I will be an artist when I grow up.

One day very early in the morning light we heard a big noise. Everyone in our village heard the loud scraping sound and came out to look. There were big machines- Papa called them bulldozers- coming toward our village. Papa and the other men of the village yelled for them to stop, but they did not stop. Mama grabbed my hand and Papa grabbed our bean pot and we ran.

All day long we hid down in the deep spaces between the big stones outside our village. I was very frightened. We covered our ears to the breaking and crushing and scrapping sounds of the bulldozers pushing our little houses down and away. Papa pulled us closer and held me and Mama tight to his chest and we listened to his heart beating strong and steady like the soft deep prayer drums. Deep inside I heard the songs from far far away.

We hid under the hot stones for a long long time. Only when it was quiet outside for many hours did Papa say it was safe to come out. Mama cried fierce silent tears when she saw the empty space where our village had been. There was nothing left behind but the sharp marks of the rough wheels in the dirt.

23

I asked Papa why they had done it. Papa said that some questions have no answers. They were just men without hope he said. They were men without the old songs. He shook his head. He reached down and picked up a handful of dirt. The dry earth sifted through his fingers. "Chante we must never lose hope."

I thought that maybe hope is like the dirt and the stars and the old songs from far far away. Perhaps hope beats strong and steady like Papa's heart and the soft deep prayer drums.

Papa made our new home under the rocks. The rain came in and bugs came in and there wasn't much room inside so Papa had to sleep outside alone.

Once again Mama cooked dark beans and rice in the big pot on the fire. The deep smell of the beans made my mouth water as I waited. Later the beans would be warm in my mouth and the rice would be sticky on my fingers and I would lick them.

When there was no food I would stay outside for a little while with Papa and we would watch the stars come out. Together we would listen to the sounds of the night, the close chirp of crickets and katydids and the far off sounds of the deep soft drumming prayers.

"Never lose hope Chante," he would say to me, "Never lose hope." I sat on the ground and made designs in the darkness with my heel. Papa whispered the old songs from far far away. I pulled my feet in and wrapped my arms around my knees and listened.

One day a man named Papa Martin came to see us. He said hello and bonjou to me and to Mama and to Papa. He spoke a little bit "piti piti" of Kreyol, the combination of African and French that we speak. Mostly he and Mama and Papa spoke with their hands and faces. He pointed to our little space under the rocks and shook his head sadly. Then he gave Mama a bucket of rice and shook Papa's hand and gave me a stick of red candy. We all smiled and smiled. The candy was the best thing I have ever eaten.

While the grown-ups talked, I sucked on the stick of candy and made designs in the dirt. I wondered if I could make the sweetness last all day.

33

Papa Martin told Mama and Papa that he was going to leave our little island of Haiti and go back to his own island called Rhode. Papa Martin said he had lots of friends in Rhode Island in a little town in the Valley of Hope. That made Papa smile. Before he left he looked at my designs in the dirt. Mama told him that I wanted to be an artist when I grow up. He nodded and smiled at me. I said "Mesi", thank you, for the candy.

All afternoon Papa sang the songs from far far away. Later we sat in silence and listened to the sounds of the night, the close chirp of crickets and katydids and the far off sounds of the deep soft drumming prayers.

When Papa Martin got back to his home in Rhode Island he spoke to his friend who was a priest, Papa Mike. Papa Mike has lots of friends, lots of grownups and lots of children. He told all of them about us! There was one little boy named Jae and a little girl named Amanda who wanted to know all about me and my artwork. He told them all about my beautiful designs in the dirt!

He talked about Mama and Papa and me and the old bean pot and the house under the rocks and the dirt and the stars. He told them my eyes were big and brown and that my hair was also brown and turning orange because there wasn't always enough to eat. Best of all, he told them that I wanted to be an artist when I grow up.

Papa Mike asked his friend Emily to talk to everyone in his Church of San Joseph about us. Emily was very shy and scared to get up in front of everyone in the church and talk to so many people. But she said that Papa Mike and God asked her to, so that was that. She told everyone in the little church that because they lived in the Valley of Hope it was time to share some of that hope with my Mama and Papa and me and all of our village friends. I think Emily was very very brave and part of forever. She is like the stars and the dirt and the old songs.

So all the people at the Church of San Joseph in the Valley of Hope in the big country of Rhode Island saved all of their extra money for a year and a day. Then they took the money and built a new village for us. They built little concrete houses with private potties for each family.

Mama cried when she first saw our new little house. I asked her why she was crying. She said that sometimes tears are happy tears. She had lots and lots of happy tears. Papa pulled us close and held me and Mama tight to his chest and we listened to his heart beating strong and steady like the soft deep prayer drums.

Deeper still I heard the songs from far far away.

Our new little house is cozy and safe. It smells of warm dark beans and rice. After the Church of San Joseph built the little houses they drilled a well so that Mama would have lots of clean water for cooking our dark beans and rice.

Then they built a community center so that I can get food and medicine and sometimes even go to school. Best of all they sent a big box of crayons just for me. On special school days I can make my designs on paper! Mama says that now, for sure, I can grow up to be an artist.

My baby brother was born in our new little house. He has big brown eyes and soft brown hair. His name is Joseph. Mama and Papa say that they named him for all the people at the Church of San Joseph in the Valley of Hope. It is our thanks to them and to God. It is the blessing of the stars and the dirt and the hope.

At night Mama holds baby Joseph close and feeds him. Papa and I sit together on the front porch and watch the stars come out. Together we listen to the sounds of the night, the close chirp of crickets and katydids and the far off sounds of the deep drumming prayers.

.

49

Often I think about the people far far away in the Valley of Hope. Papa says that they too can see the stars. Papa says that we are all part of forever like the old songs. I smile in the darkness. I know that both here and there hope beats strong and steady.